"Keep Christmas with You
All Through the Year"

Music by Sam Pottle

Lyrics by David Axlerod

Library of Congress Cataloging in Publication Data: Stone, Jon. Christmas Eve on Sesame Street. SUMMARY: On Christmas Eve the Sesame Street friends exchange gifts, go skating, worry about Santa, and write their wish list. [1. Christmas stories] I. Sesame Street (Television program) II. Title. PZ7.S87785Ch [E] 81-50247 AACR2 ISBN: 0-394-84733-4

Manufactured in the United States of America   5 6 7 8 9 0

Christmas Eve on Sesame Street

Created by Jon Stone
Illustrated by Joe Mathieu

Based on the television special
"Christmas Eve on Sesame Street"
written by Jon Stone and Joseph A. Bailey

On Sesame Street, Susan is performed
by Loretta Long, Gordon by Roscoe Orman, David
by Northern Calloway, Olivia by Alaina
Reed, Mr. Hooper by Will Lee, Maria by Sonia
Manzano, and Bob by Bob McGrath.

Random House / Children's Television Workshop

It was the afternoon of Christmas Eve, and some friends from Sesame Street were having a skating party.

"Let's play snap-the-whip!"
said Cookie Monster.
"Wonderful! Wonderful!
One time around!" said the
Count.

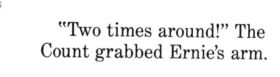

"Two times around!" The
Count grabbed Ernie's arm.

"Three times
around!" the
Count continued.
Ernie took Bert's
arm and spun him
around.

"Four times around! Five times around!" The Count was
delighted, but Bert grabbed desperately at a trash can that just
happened to be skating by.

From inside the can a grouchy voice grumbled, "Hey, take your hands off the hardware!"

"Six times around!" yelled the Count.

"Take it easy!" yelled the trash can.

"Stop!" yelled Bert.

But now they were going too fast to stop. Around and around and around, faster and faster and faster! Bert tried with all his might to hold on, but . . .

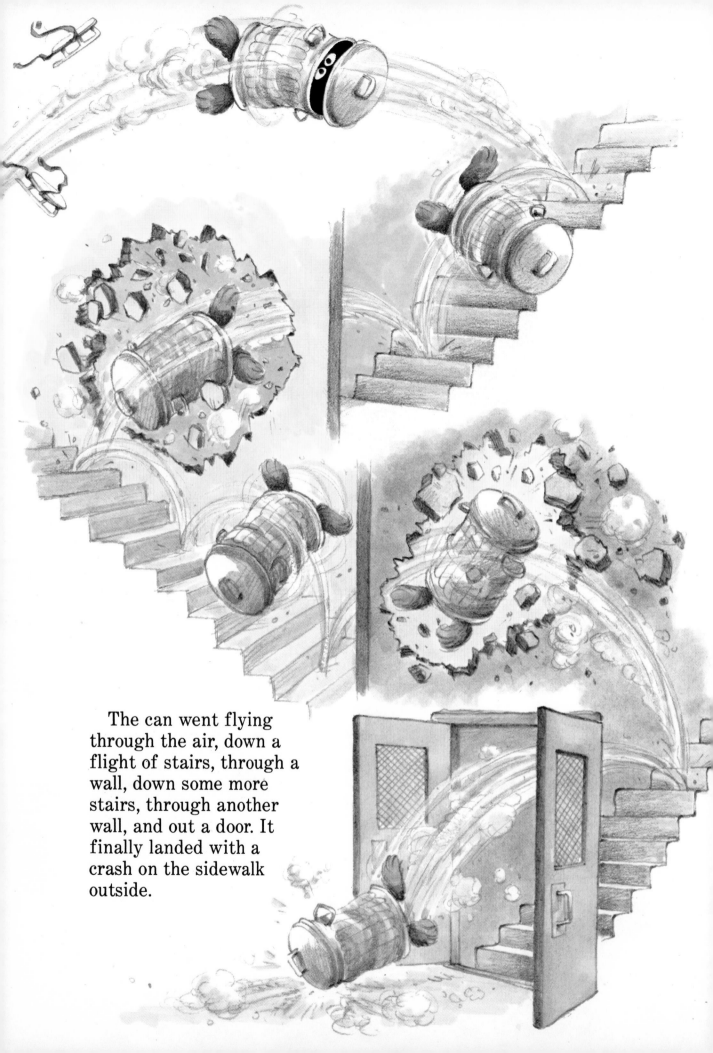

The can went flying
through the air, down a
flight of stairs, through a
wall, down some more
stairs, through another
wall, and out a door. It
finally landed with a
crash on the sidewalk
outside.

"Oscar, are you all right?" Big Bird set the trash can upright. Oscar poked his head out and shook his green fur.

"All right?! Let's go back and do it again!" Then he mumbled, "I've been thrown out of better places than that."

"Oh, I'm so glad you're all right, Oscar," said Big Bird. "I want everybody to be happy on Christmas Eve. It's a big night tonight. Santa's reindeer will be landing on the roof, and then he'll take his big bag of toys and slide right down the chimney!"

Oscar couldn't stand it.

"Just hold it right there, birdbrain. Do you know how big the inside of a chimney is?"

Big Bird and his friend Patty didn't.

"About this big, that's how big." Oscar held his grubby paws about six inches apart. "So how's a guy like Santa Claus, who's built like a dump truck, how's he going to get down all those skinny chimneys? Huh?"

Big Bird had to think about that.

"Well, he holds his breath, like this . . ." Big Bird sucked in his breath to make himself thinner.

"That's like trying to get a basketball into a ginger-ale bottle!" snorted Oscar.

Big Bird tried again: "Well, he could come down the fire escape and in the window."

"Window's locked!" growled Oscar.

"Through the door?" asked Patty.

"Door's locked!" snapped Oscar.

Big Bird's eyes filled with tears.

"I don't know *how* Santa gets in. . . ."

Then Oscar spoke very softly, so Big Bird and Patty had to lean close to hear him.

"Well, I think you'd better find *out!* Because if there isn't a way for him to get in, there are going to be a lot of empty stockings around town tomorrow morning. Heh, heh, heh.

"Merry Christmas."

Big Bird sighed and sat down on the curb. He
was so upset that he didn't notice his friends were
heading back to Sesame Street. They were singing
and laughing, but Big Bird didn't even hear them.

"Come on, Big Bird," said Patty. "It's time to go
home."

When Big Bird and Patty finally arrived back on Sesame Street, Kermit the Frog was waiting for them. Kermit could see right away that something was wrong. And being a clever frog, he knew just how to find out what was wrong.

"What's wrong?" he asked.

Big Bird told him. "Oh, it's that Oscar. Everything was fine until he started asking 'How does Santa Claus get down those skinny chimneys when he's so fat?'"

"And we've got to find out," said Patty.

Big Bird agreed. "Because if Santa can't get down the chimney, nobody will get any presents tonight!"

Now Kermit knew that was wrong, and he gave the problem some frogthought. Then he had a frogidea!

"Who knows more about Santa Claus than anybody?"

Big Bird and Patty guessed. "The elves?"

"Mrs. Claus?"

"Macy's?"

But Kermit had another answer. "Kids! That's who. So I'll just round up Grover and Herry and we'll go and ask some kids!" And off he went to find Grover and Herry.

In the basement apartment at 123 Sesame Street, Ernie threw his skates under the sofa. Bert was already undressed and ready for a hot bath.

"Ohhh boy," he sighed as he slowly lowered himself into the bubbles. "This feels peachy."

But suddenly he had a terrible thought. "Golly wonkers! It's Christmas Eve, and I still don't have an idea for Ernie's present. It's got to be something special. Wait a minute! What's this in the tub?" He groped around and fished out a chubby little bathtub toy. "It's Ernie's Rubber Duckie. Say, that gives me a nifty idea! I know what to get Ernie. I'll get him a soap dish. He can put his Rubber Duckie in it so it won't keep falling into the water. I'd better get over to Mr. Hooper's store right away."

Meanwhile, in the living room, Ernie noticed something shiny on the rug. Because he was curious, he did something that he almost never did. He picked it up.

"Why, it's a paper clip," he said. "I'll bet it's from my old buddy Bert's paper-clip collection." He looked closer. "Of course. It's Bert's 1957 Acme. Why, he'd feel just awful if he lost this.

"Hey! Now I know what I'll get Bert for Christmas! I'll get him a cigar box so he can keep his paper-clip collection in it. That's what I'll get him. Then none of his paper clips will ever get lost again."

As soon as Bert left the bathroom, Ernie grabbed Rubber Duckie.

"Bert," called Ernie, "I'm going out for a while." He tossed the 1957 Acme paper clip over his shoulder, back onto the rug, and marched out the front door.

Ernie hurried to Mr. Hooper's store.

"Well, hello, Ernie," said Mr. Hooper. "What brings you here?"

"Hi there, Mr. Hooper," said Ernie. "Just doing a little last-minute Christmas shopping." Then he spotted just the thing he was looking for. "Say, that sure is a fine-looking cigar box on your shelf. I don't have any money, Mr. Hooper, but suppose I gave you Rubber Duckie here for that cigar box? Would you trade?"

"Ernie!" exclaimed Mr. Hooper. He couldn't believe his ears. "Are you sure? You love that Rubber Duckie more than anything!"

Ernie swallowed hard and looked up at Mr. Hooper. "I've just got to have that cigar box."

Mr. Hooper stared long and hard at the sad little face, then slowly took the cigar box down from the shelf.

"Well, if it's really that important . . ." he said. "Here's the cigar box, Ernie."

"Thanks, Mr. Hooper," said Ernie. "And here's Rubber Duckie." He thought for a moment. "Good-bye, Mr. Hooper." Then he looked one last time at his chubby little yellow bathtub friend and said the hardest thing in the world for him to say. "Good-bye, Rubber Duckie."

As Ernie turned to leave, the door opened. It was Bert! Ernie quickly hid the cigar box behind his back.

"Errr . . . See you at home, Bert," he said. And before Bert could answer, Ernie ran out of Mr. Hooper's store, holding the cigar box so Bert couldn't see it.

"Ahem . . . Mr. Hooper!" stammered Bert, "I am prepared to offer you the deal of a lifetime. Now, this is the finest paper-clip collection in the free world. Just look. Oh, here's my chrome-plated Jumbo Gem. Ah, and this is the one I bent in the shape of the letter W! Ah . . ."

"It's very impressive, Bert," said Mr. Hooper.

Bert agreed. "Yes, and they're all so . . . individual. Mr. Hooper, I am prepared to trade you this terrific paper-clip collection for just one small soap dish. What do you say, Mr. Hooper? Do we have a deal?"

Mr. Hooper knew how Bert felt about his paper-clip collection. It was very much the same way Ernie felt about his Rubber Duckie, but he could see that Bert's mind was made up.

"What can I say, Bert? You talked me into it. Here's the soap dish. I'll put it in a nice box for you."

"Oh, thank you, Mr. Hooper!" Then Bert paused for a moment. "There's just one more thing, Mr. Hooper. Could I come by once in a while and look at my paper—" His voice choked and his eyes filled with tears. He couldn't finish the question. "Never mind," he said. Bert slowly turned his back on the paper clips and left the store.

Mr. Hooper stared after his
friend. Then he looked down at
the Rubber Duckie and paper
clips on his counter. After a
moment he smiled, gathered
them up and put them in boxes,
and closed his shop. He hurried
down Sesame Street. He was
thinking so hard he didn't even
notice Bob until Bob spoke to him.
   "Happy Chanukah, Mr. Hooper."
   It was just like Bob to
remember that Mr. Hooper
celebrated the Jewish holiday at
this time of the year. "Thank
you, Bob," he said, "and Merry
Christmas to you."

As Mr. Hooper passed the trash cans in front of 123 Sesame Street, he heard a gravelly, grouchy voice.

"Chanukah, Christmas, presents, songs, happy kids . . . it's all a lot of baloney, if you ask me." Mr. Hooper stopped and thoughtfully touched the ratty grouch stocking that was hanging from Oscar's can.

"If it's all a lot of baloney, Oscar," he asked, "then why do you have this stocking hung here on Christmas Eve?"

Oscar was trapped, but he managed to think fast.

"If you *must* know, Mr. Nosey Parker, I was just drying my laundry!"

And Oscar slammed back into his can so Mr. Hooper couldn't see how embarrassed he was.

After Ernie had left Mr. Hooper's store, he went right home and wrapped Bert's present. And just in time, too. As he was taping the last corner, Bert walked in the door.

"Oh, I'm glad you're home, Bert, old Buddy," said Ernie. "I can't stand it any longer! Let's open our presents right now."

"Okay, Ernie," said Bert. "Let's go." He handed Ernie the package he was carrying.

"Merry Christmas, Ernie."

"Merry Christmas, Bert. You go first."

Bert studied the neatly wrapped present that Ernie held out to him. "Ernie, what a superb wrapping job! Now, if I can just slide my finger under the paper and get the tape. . . . No. How about a scissors? Well, maybe if I just . . ."

Ernie couldn't stand waiting. "Just open it, Bert!" he howled, and Bert tore off the paper.

"Oh, hunky-dory, Ernie. A cigar box!"

"It's for your paper-clip collection, Bert."

Suddenly Bert's knees became weak and his face felt cold and clammy. "For my paper clips?" Tears filled his big round eyes, but somehow he controlled himself.

"Oh . . . ah . . . er . . . yah . . . well. . . . Why don't you open your present, Ernie?"

And Ernie did. "Why, Bert! It's a soap dish!"

"That's right, Ernie," Bert said proudly. "I got it for Rubber Duckie!"

As soon as Ernie heard it was for Rubber Duckie, his heart just broke. Now there would always be an empty soap dish in his tubby to remind him that Rubber Duckie was gone forever.

Just then there was a knock at the door.

"Come in," Ernie said sadly.

It was Mr. Hooper.

"Merry Christmas, boys," he said, and he handed a gift to each of them. Ernie and Bert tried to smile. Slowly they unwrapped the presents, not really caring what was inside. Not really caring, that is, until they *saw* what was inside. Bert reached into the wrapping and pulled out a handful of bright, shiny metal.

"Mr. Hooper!" he exclaimed. "It's my paper-clip collection!"

"And here's my Rubber Duckie!" shouted Ernie, jumping up and down. But suddenly Bert had a terrible thought.

"Ernie, we didn't get Mr. Hooper anything."

"You're wrong, Bert," said Mr. Hooper. "I got the best Christmas present ever. My present was seeing that everyone got exactly what he wanted for Christmas!"

Kermit and Herry and Grover were spending the afternoon talking to kids.

Everyone they asked had a different idea about how Santa Claus gets down the chimney, and Kermit wrote down every single answer.

Finally, Kermit went back to where Big Bird, Patty, and Snuffy were waiting.

"It doesn't look good, Big Bird," he said. "Just listen to some of the answers we got.

"Santa Claus goes on a crash diet every Christmas Eve and loses two hundred pounds.

"Several kids believe that they have rubber chimneys.

"Here's one who says Santa either has a fishing pole or very long arms.

"A boy on Seventy-second Street thinks Santa sends one of his elves.

"Or how about this? He sneaks in with the relatives at Thanksgiving and hides in the laundry room until Christmas."

"No, no, no," moaned Big Bird. "This isn't getting us anywhere! Here it is Christmas Eve and we still don't know how Santa gets down the chimney. What are we going to do?"

"I'm really sorry, Big Bird," said Kermit, "but we tried."

"Well, what do *you* think, Kermit?" asked Big Bird.

"Me? Oh, I think he ... uh ... maybe what he does is ..." Kermit stopped and thought for a long time.

"I don't know *how* Santa gets down the chimney, Big Bird."

Patty and Big Bird were left alone with Snuffy.

"Now, Snuffy," said Big Bird, "we're going to use the scientific way to find out how big fat Santa gets down those skinny little chimneys."

"I'm sure it will work if you thought of it, Bird," said Snuffy.

"Now here's what we'll do," continued Big Bird. "You play the part of Santa Claus, and we'll pretend that this barrel is a chimney!"

"Okay, Bird," said Snuffy. "Ho, ho, ho!"

"Now let's see," said Big Bird. "You put one foot down in the barrel..." Snuffy did. "And now the other foot. And now another foot..."

"I don't think Santa has more than two feet, Bird," said Snuffy.

Big Bird considered that and came up with a typical bird answer. "Well, just pretend he has a reindeer with him."

Snuffy thought that made sense.

"Bird," he said, putting his fourth foot into the barrel, "it's getting harder to 'Ho Ho Ho.'"

Big Bird stood back and studied his friend, who looked very worried with all four of his legs stuffed tightly into a very small barrel. Suddenly, Big Bird burst into a delighted smile.

"Snuffy! Maybe that's how Santa Claus gets into the chimney!"

"There's just one thing, Bird..." Snuffy said sadly. "Do we know how he gets *out*?"

It was getting dark, and Patty and Big Bird still didn't know how Santa would get down the chimney. Snuffy lumbered home to his cave, leaving his two friends cuddled together in the nest. Patty snuggled up into the yellow feathers to keep warm, and she and Big Bird thought very hard for a long time. Large snowflakes began falling.

"You'd better go home, Patty," Big Bird said. "It's starting to snow."

Patty climbed out of the nest and stared at her friend. He looked so sad. What could she say to cheer him up?

"Don't worry, Big Bird. Even if we *don't* know how, Santa will come down the chimney. Really he will."

"Oh no," said Big Bird. "It'll never work."

Patty took a few steps but decided to give it one more try. She turned back to the bird and said the happiest thing she could think of.

"Merry Christmas."

But Big Bird didn't even look up. Patty shook her head and left.

"Wait a minute," Big Bird said to himself. "I can find out how Santa gets down those itty-bitty chimneys!"

Big Bird climbed out of his nest, marched past Oscar's can, into Gordon and Susan's house, and up five flights of stairs. Then he poked his beak out the door to the snow-covered roof. No one was there but Bert's pigeons.

"Hi, fellas," he said. "How are things up here on the roof? You haven't seen Santa Claus, have you?" The pigeons cooed no.

"There's our skinny little chimney!" said Big Bird. "I'm just going to stay here and *watch* how Santa gets down that little thing. Brrrrr! It is *cold!* I don't see how those penguins can take it!"

He pulled up a box, brushed the snow off of it, and sat down, staring very hard at the chimney.

He tried his best not to look away even once, but with the soft snow falling and the gentle cooing of the pigeons, he grew sleepier . . . and sleepier . . . and sleepier.

Down in the Fixit Shop, Cookie Monster was getting ready to write a note to Santa Claus. He had borrowed a piece of paper and a great big pencil from Luis, and he began to write.

"Dear Sandy..."

Then he thought out loud. "Oh, what me ask for? What else? COOKIES! Oh yeah, yeah, yeah. Two dozen coconut macaroons. NO-no-no-no. Maybe pound and a half of figgy newtons! Ohhh, me getting so HUNGRY!"

And without realizing what he was doing, Cookie Monster took a big bite out of his pencil.

"Me *love* cookies! Oatmeal cookies! Me ask for three dozen ... Oh, what the hey ... FOUR dozen!"

And he took another bite of his pencil.

"Or how about banana cookies? Or prune cookies? Chocolate-covered-marshmallow-with-jelly-inside cookies?"

He stuffed the rest of the pencil, eraser and all, into his mouth and ate it.

"Me got to write that down."

And he looked up, down, and all around.

"Where pencil?" he asked.

Cookie Monster moved over to Luis' typewriter and rolled a sheet of paper into it. Since he'd lost his pencil, he would type his letter.

"Dear Sandy Claus," he typed slowly. "Me no care *what* kind of cookies you bring me. You surprise Cookie Monster."

Then he began to daydream again.

"Boy, me wonder what Sandy Claus going to bring me . . . maybe coconut fudge cookies."

He absent-mindedly played with the typewriter keys.

"Or dainty little raisin cookies. Me LOVE raisin cookies!"

He ripped a handful of little keys off the typewriter and stuffed them into his mouth.

"Or maybe Sandy bring me bunch of fortune cookies with delicious paper inside."

And without thinking, he tore the roller off the typewriter and ate it, along with the paper he was going to type on.

"Delicious! Or Sandy bring *round* cookies!"

He ate the two little round spools that held the typewriter ribbon.

"Cowabunga!" he howled as he whomped the rest of the typewriter and ate the pieces. Then he looked up, down, and all around.

"Where typewriter?"

Cookie Monster moved over to Luis' telephone and said to himself, "Christmas Eve too late for letter to Sandy Claus anyway, so me *call* him. Let's see . . . North Pole area code . . ." He began to dial the number, and as he dialed he thought of what he would say when Santa answered.

"Oh boy, oh boy, oh boy. Me get him on phone and say, 'Hi, Sandy Claus! Cookie Monster here!' And then me ask him to bring me . . ."

He held the telephone and stared lovingly at the receiver as he spoke.

"Bring me two . . . delicious, round, chocolate, fudge-covered . . . CUPPYCAKES!!!"

And he ate the telephone that looked for all the world like two delicious, round, chocolate, fudge-covered cuppycakes. After a moment he heard a click in his tummy. Then he heard a voice coming from deep inside him.

"Ho! Ho! Ho! Hello . . . hello?"

Cookie slowly realized what he had done.

"Oh boy. Me better go see Gordon. He always know what to do."

Up in Gordon and Susan's apartment, Gordon was hanging the Christmas stockings. Cookie followed him around as he worked.

"Gordon! Me tried to write letter to Sandy Claus but me ate pencil. Me ate typewriter, too!"

"Well, Santa knows all about you, Cookie Monster," laughed Gordon. "He'll bring you some cookies."

"Then me tried to call Sandy. But telephone look like cuppycakes and me ate it, too! Sandy never bring Cookie Monster cookies now!"

"Yes, he will, Cookie Monster. But it might be a good idea if you left him a little something."

"That terrific idea," said Cookie. "Sandy Claus leave me cookies and me leave Sandy . . . necktie!" Then he had a better idea. "No-no-no! Me leave him . . . shaving cream!"

"Well, you could. But most people leave him . . ."

"What? What?" Cookie Monster could hardly wait to hear. "What do most people leave for Sandy Claus?"

"Cookies," Gordon said quietly.

Cookie Monster fainted.

Gordon thought he heard something. It might have been someone knocking, but it was so soft that he wasn't sure. He went to the door and opened it. Patty was standing in the hallway, her eyes filled with tears.

"Big Bird's gone! He was acting so funny when I left him that I went back to his nest to see him—and he was *gone!*"

Gordon tried not to look worried. He stood up and called to Susan to get her coat. Then he turned back to Patty and said, "Don't worry. We'll find him."

He and Cookie and Susan and Patty hurried down to the street to find Big Bird. Bob and Mr. Hooper, Linda, Maria, and Olivia all joined in the search.

All the while his friends were searching for him,
Big Bird was sound asleep on the roof.

"Oscar," Maria said, "I hope you're satisfied. You had to start all that stuff about Santa and tiny chimneys and no presents, and you've upset Big Bird so much that he's gone."

"Aw, I was only teasing him," Oscar answered. "He'll come back. He's part homing pigeon. Besides, what's the big deal? He lives outdoors anyway."

"Now, look here, Oscar." Maria was getting angry. "His nest is something different. That's Big Bird's home. He's got his electric blanket there, and heating pads, and he's near all the people who love him. But it's Christmas Eve and he's out there somewhere in this big city. It's snowing and getting colder and he could be in serious trouble unless we find him."

"Okay, okay," Oscar said, "let's go."

Now *everyone* on Sesame Street
was looking for Big Bird.

Up on the cold roof, Big Bird was fast asleep. Snow was piling up around his feet, and two little icicles had formed on his beak. He was in danger of freezing, but *he* didn't know that. He was dreaming the nicest dream. . . . He could hear the jingle of sleigh bells and the clatter of reindeer hooves landing on the roof.

But maybe it wasn't a dream. Maybe it was really happening. Or maybe it was just the noises from the street below. . . .

Then Big Bird dreamed that someone was jumping down from the sleigh and walking closer and closer to him. No, that was just the wind blowing through the chimneys. Or was it the pigeons fluttering in their pigeon coop?

But it seemed so real. . . .

And then this big, fat, jolly fellow was standing right in front of him. He reached down and touched Big Bird to wake him up.

Or maybe it was just some snow blowing against his feathers. But whatever it was, Big Bird's eyes suddenly opened.

Big Bird looked all around the roof, but no one was there. There wasn't even a footprint in the snow. He shook his feathers and shivered.

"Brrrr. Is it cold!" he said. "I'd better go down to Gordon and Susan's and warm up."

He poked himself in the side. "I think I froze my giblets!"

Big Bird climbed down the stairs to Susan's apartment.

When Patty caught sight of him, she shrieked and giggled and buried herself in his feathers.

"Big Bird! Are you all right?" asked Susan.

"Oh y-y-yes," he stammered, "except for my giblets."

"Where have you been?" asked Gordon.

"Well," said Big Bird, "I went up on the roof to see if I could see Santa Claus. But then I fell asleep. Brrrr! I got so cold that I came down to get warm. But I'm going right back up there!"

"Oh no, you're not!" said Gordon. "You're going to come into our apartment and thaw out!"

"But I can't, Gordon! I'll miss Santa!"

"Yes, you can! Now come on!"

Gordon pulled Big Bird through the doorway into the warm apartment.

Now Gordon and Susan's living room looked like fairyland. The tree twinkled with colored lights. Gifts were piled high under its branches. The stockings bulged with presents, and holly and mistletoe and ribbons and tinsel hung everywhere.

Big Bird stopped and stared at the beautiful room.

"Oh, dear," he sighed. "Now I'll *never* find out how Santa did it!"

Gordon looked at his friend. "Big Bird, do you remember what Oscar said to you?"

"Yes," Big Bird answered. "Oscar said that if Santa Claus couldn't get down those itty-bitty chimneys no one would get any presents."

"Well, just look around," Gordon said. "Does it look like no one's getting any presents?"

"No," answered Big Bird, his eyes getting wider as he looked around the room. "But it's a miracle! How did he do it?"

"Why do you want to know, Big Bird?"

"Well, Gordon, it's important."

"No, Big Bird. That's not what's important," Gordon said. "What's important is that we lost you tonight, and we were all very worried about you. And now you're back safe and sound, and we're all together for Christmas. That's what's important."

Suddenly the door burst open. It was Oscar.

"Heh, heh. I hear the turkey's back."

"Hi there, Oscar," said Big Bird.

"Listen, you big canary," grumbled Oscar, "I'm glad you're back ... because I want to ask you a question."

Big Bird leaned low so he could hear what Oscar wanted to ask, and Oscar let him have it.

"How do you think the Easter Bunny can hide all those eggs in one night?"

Gordon gave Oscar's can a good solid whack on the lid. From inside, Oscar laughed.

"Come on outside, Big Bird," said Gordon. "Let's go tell everyone you're all right."

Patty held tight to Big Bird's feathers to make sure he wouldn't get lost again, and they all went out to celebrate Christmas Eve on Sesame Street.

"True Blue Miracle"

Music and lyrics by Carol Hall

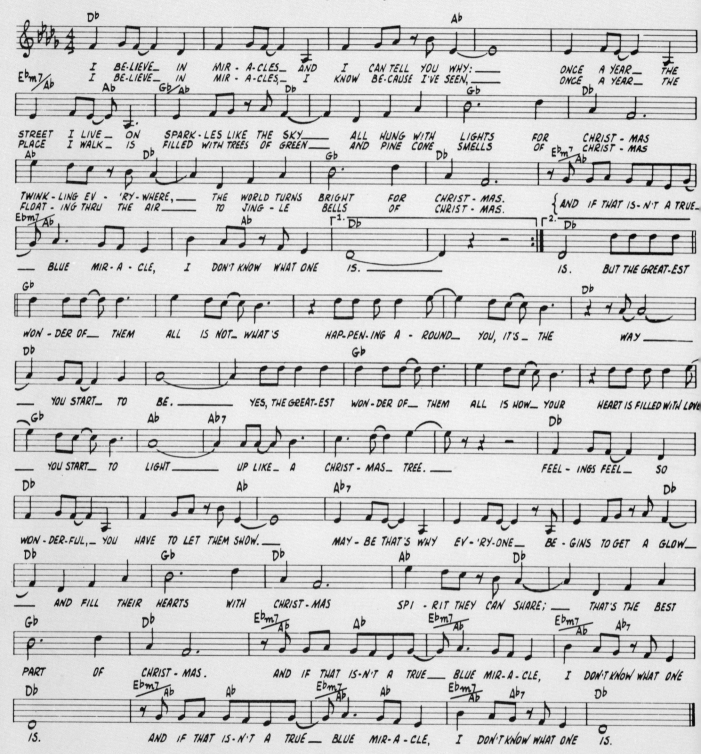